The Passion of Valentino Santi

Written, Arranged, & Composed By
Dé Avery La Monte Priest

 TM

LUPA PRESS

Minneapolis, Minnesota

The Passion of Valentino Santi

lupapress@zoho.com
www.deaverypriest.com

Front cover photo by Persephone P. Priest
of *Grotesque* - detail from the base of Perseus with the
Head of Medusa, Cellini, Firenze, 2008

Author photo by Persephone P. Priest
of the author, son of a golden jackal, 2017

Printed in the United States of America

4 Velma & Phillis
(disjointed sibyls en their own right)

<u>Special Thanks 2</u>
Persephone
(4 being a beautiful muse),
Cher
(4 the push),
Zelda Sayre Fitzgerald
(4 a heartbreakingly beautiful life),
Carol Burling
(4 the first read and true title),
Travis Bickle
(4 being a dark & disturbed hero of the wasteland),
The Valerio Family
(4 the name Valentino)

&

Prince Rogers Nelson
(4 the spark)

iv

CONTENTS

Scenes from The Wasteland

How the War Was Won

How the Wasteland Came 2 Be

Nota Bene № 1

So Much Paper On The Walls •
So Much Lambskin Lining The Halls Of
Mystic Scholars • I Read What They Said • I Read What
They Wrote • I Read It All •
Cups Of Gold Pinched • Forced Maidens •
Swords And Stones And Knightly Conquest •

I Read It All • And All Of It Rubbish! •

I Turned 7 In The Spring Of '49 •
The Year The Oceans Dried Up • The Year The Flow Of
Rivers By Unseen Hands Was Stemmed And The Lakes
Nearly Vanished •
In The Spring Of '49 I turned 7 • The Year Everything
And Everyone Came Undone •

- Valentino Santi

Fanfare / Wasteland

Two fingers stroke her cheek
As blood rushes from the crown of her head
To the width of her hips

Two fingers, slender and pale,
Press her cup / Its lips

Awakening Monsters
Stirring her Sex

Dizzy,

She wrenches the bed sheets
Until her candle wax drips
And a pool of ambrosia puddles

(Ento the palm of his hand)

Kickoff yur shoes
Unbelt yur pants

Clumsily, he does
No such thing

Clumsily, he brandishes
His grandmother's pinking shears

[Aside.]
A Ravager of the Body,
A Ravager of the Soul (en his mind's eye).

{**Tambourine Scroll**}

Its blades do not disappoint
                or despair
Tho' he makes a mess of things
And,

En haste,

Carves her young, tender flesh where he ought not

(The stink of a ruptured kidney chokes the aire)

{Trumpets Blow And Trumpets Blare}

Do not panic!

Do not be alarmed
When eye stiffen my collar, link my cuffs
And tell you, *We are damned!*

{Drum Roll}

Welcome friend! (or foe)
Welcome to Palaces of Desolation
And Damnation

Welcome to Love's last breath
                Love's tyrannous ruin
                Love's
Most epic death

Welcome cowherd
To yur last stop

Welcome blacksmith
To yur cold, cold hearth

Welcome courtesan
To yur rotting frock

Welcome one and all!
To yur smashed windmills

   yur long, lost
Misguided quest

   yur dry well

   yur desert
   yur broken soul
(At ancient behest)

Welcome, welcome
One and all

Welcome to Shambhala
(Struck down!)

Welcome
One and all
To the Wasteland

Nota Bene № 2

We Didn't Feed Love And It Went Away •
And When Love Went Away The Water Went With It •
We Didn't Feed Love • We Didn't Keep It Well Fed •
Didn't Keep It Strong • We Didn't Make Its Wellbeing A
High Priority And Everything Went Horribly Wrong • We
Stopped Opening Doors And Started Strangling Whores •
We Stopped Standing When Our Wives Entered Rooms
And Our Daughters Jumped Brooms • We Didn't Feed
Love And It Went Away • And When Love Went Away
The Water Went With It • We Didn't Feed Love • We
Didn't Keep It Well Fed •
We Stopped Pruning Grandma's Orchids • We Stopped
Raking Her Leaves • Stopped Saying Thank You •
Stopped Saying Please •

We Stopped Caring Ya'll • Stopped Getting Naked •
Stopped Holding Hands • For Fear Of Judgment • For Fear
Of The Sadists Who Walk Freely Among Us •
Who Cream Their Britches When They Are Met With
Despair And The Cremation Of Care • We Didn't Feed
Love And It Went Away • And When Love Went Away
The Water Went With It • We Didn't Feed Love • We
Didn't Keep It Well Fed • Our Brothers We Cut Down •
Our Sisters We Caged • Our Cousins We Tied To Railroad
Tracks Without Tenderness • And Without Tenderness We
Aged • We Stopped Walking • Stopped Talking •
Old School I Know • We Stopped Reading The Psalms
Auntie Taught Us • Old School I Know •

- Valentino Santi

Night of the Broken Glass

What were you doing when the bombs fell?
(Did you hear the blast?)

Where were you when you heard the news?
(Did you see the flash   .   .   .   of Light?)

They said 400 oceans were lost

{One-Beat Pause}

What shoes were you wearing
When the vigor of Shambhala wither'd and
The god-of-the-hinge lay bleeding en the grove?

What booze capped your flask
When they boarded the Wells
And constructed the Presses?

What beads did you hold
When the crematorium fyres raged
Across the countryside?

They said 400 cedars were lost

{Fingercymbals-Twice}

So,
What were you doing when their soot rose
And blacken'd the Sun?

O,
How did you breathe the aire? / *That* aire?
An aire sickened sweetly with Death?

{One-Beat Pause}

What prayers did you pray
When they stole Greenbaum's little girl straight away?
When they found her trembling en the pantry?

When they drew her from her home,
Bruised her shoulder
And   bolder

Still

Stained her Rose
And dumped her body
En a deep furrow outside the city walls?

{Two-Beat Pause}

What declarations did you sign
When the Lizards stole golden cups
From whyte fingers long and fine?

What songs did you sing?

{Fingercymbals-Twice}

What songs
When the band chose to play?

When Baghdad became a desert
And Love got en the way
Of that barren, desolate thing?

So,
What songs?
What songs did you sing?

Nota Bene № 3

Tiger Tiger Burning Bright •
Shower Him With Flowers (From TheGardenOfAdonis) •
Shower Him With Light • So A Dreamer Of Days
May Contemplate The Present Age In Black
And White:

Regrettably We Are A Species Without Recourse • And
Need Not Concern Ourselves With Daggers And Demons •
Rape Murder And Magick • Monstrous Are We •
Through And Through •
Our Deeds • Our Lead • Our Fears • Our Mead •

- Valentino Santi

Strange Little Girl

Who among us is not haunted
By a lock of perfumed hair
Or a piano concerto en D minor?

Who among us is not tormented
By a nightly recollection of some face
                              some place

                    some grotesque moment
                    en tyme

A moment held too tightly
For far   too long
Until its waters,
Once the sands of Dreaming
Once the sweet elixir of Life,

Become stagnant and poisonous

Alas!
Who among us does not pray routinely
For redemption, rebirth and escape
From unspeakable cruelties self-inflicted?

For this reason
And this reason alone

My long and arduous journey begins en haste
(On a frosty December morn)

Outside the palace walls
A mile or two up the road
Where the ancient battlements once stood

My journey Westward
My journey en pursuit
Of a glorious wonder (from the dayes of olde)

. . . traveling (as eye sometymes do)
Without the pow'rs and privileges
Afforded a beast of my rank
            a beast
Born to the golden bough

My presence
Among the flora and fauna
Goes unnoticed

No sterling crown, sistahs
No glass scepter, brothas
No robes of purple, red, and gold

It's been dayes
Since the tracks of a desert hare crossed my path
Or the musk of a whyte antelope fill'd my nostrils

Note the ribcage
(Now visible beneath a scrawny, y'llow hide)

Note the mane, dull and matted
(Now obscuring sunken, lethargic eyes)

{One-Beat Pause}

Beyond the cleric's garten of stone
Water is scarce and game
Even   scarcer

But it matters not (my stomach stopped growling
            quitesometyme ago)

Note the paws
(Now caked with blood)
And the grimace accompanying a once princely gait

Ev'ry step, brothas
Feels like a step bare
Atop broken glass

As my life / most recently / the life of a King
Who fill'd his cup, his bed, his pride, his poison ring
My life / most recently / rid of forethought / rid of poverty /
rid of blight

The life of a brier rose / the life of a star engulf 'd by light

Safe and remote

Has made me soft
And tender under foot

[Soft Aside.]
Momentary bliss, Brothas, momentary bliss.
Surely not for the faint of Heart.

Beyond the reach of my mettle
Beyond the reach of my desires and fears
There is a land laid waste
a land laid low

Beyond the sibyl's bless-ed wood
Beyond the mark of my best archer's bow

It rises to split the hem
Of the poor wretch (a wretch such as eye)
Who finds himself lightyears away from grace

Beyond the reach of the starling's song,
Her greenish-black pearl
Her crescendo
Her face / Her shore

Note the limp
(A remnant of the many misfortunes met by one
Brave enough / Fool enough
To embark upon a crossing such as this)

It lingers still
Tho' it has been a fortnight since the hyenas' attack,
Brutal and unprovoked

Note the hip
It aches still
Tho' the left hind quarter has healed nicely

Alas! It aches
Whenever, at eventide, the desert winds choose
To carry a Northerly chill

En the distance,
The ruins of Valhalla make themselves known to me

Statues of quartz embedded stone
(The graveyard's graveyard!)

Many of them broken (like the pieta of Mary's son)
Many of the them beheaded (like the bust of Alexander /
                                    like the Hun)

Some are entact (like the eldest, Prometheus bound)
And some are powder (like the wizard Faust
                              and his Hellhound)

{Two-Beat Pause}

When eye reach the ramparts of the Garten City
Poseidon (so the story goes)
Rises from the oceanic steppes of Atlantis
And hurls his trident ento the Sun

The skyes darken

A clapofthunder and
A flashoflightning follow

Whereby an entrance is illuminated

{One-Beat Pause}

Eye hesitate

[Indecipherable Whispers.]

Afraid! Of whom or what am eye afraid?

Accused, eye stand

And alas . . . guilty, eye am

{Two-Beat Pause}

Afraid

Of nightmares transparent and the terror they beget
When the belly is empty and the bones are at rest
And the brain is laden with a mad blur of thoughts
And pictures,
Disjointed snapshots of athousand lives lived
                              athousand Wastelands endured

Some kind (to the soul)
Some . . . not so kind

[Soft Aside.]
When the nightmares come
And fill yur skull's empty spaces
With light and shadow

You know where you stand or if
You   stand
A'tall.

But fear is not the reason why
My legs take root
And then turn to stone

This you **must** understand and
This you must know:

Ev'ry nursery rime
Read aloud to me
Whilst eye drank from my Mother's lap

Was read aloud
En preparation for this daye

Ev'ry tome
Ev'ry epic poem

Ev'ry charm ceremoniously spat
Onto parchment

Ev'ry red lyrical rose
Ev'ry myth taught me was
Taught en preparation for this hour

The hour
When eye,

A King of Kings
of stately palaces
And the comforts they bring,

Arrive at the Garten City

And here

It lies

B'fore me

Between the pillars of Solomon
the pillars of Hermes

And here
Their songs / the same song

songs of Death
songs of Salvation
Like athousand lashes sharp behind the eyes

Burn

{**One-Beat Pause**}

The songs of athousand Indras
athousand Kings

athousand Caliphs
athousand Wings

Alas! Eye am not unique
(Groaning en travail)
Alas! Eye am not alone
(With my bruised ego / My crooked tail)

They too
Felt the boot heels of Atlas dig ento their brow

They too
Felt the blush of embarrassment en their cheeks
Upon knowing
They weren't the first to make this journey
And neither would they be the last

They too
Felt their envy exposed

And paws nailed
To this immovable spot
To this place
Desolate and sorrowful

Yea

They too heard the arias
Of monarchs past

And
They too hesitated at the pillars of Solomon
                    the pillars of Hermes

And they too stood where eye now stand
Groaning en travail, *Eye am neither the first*
                    nor shall eye be the last!

Like those b'fore me,
Eye break the barrier of the Garten City
And watch as a firelight falls upon her face

This strange little girl
Whose coat reeks of brimstone and
Whose pouty lips, when wet,
Part (ever so slowly) to converse with the dead

She does not see me crouch en the thorn bush
She does not hear me groom my tail

Desperate tho' eye am to fall soft-ly ento her hair and
Taste longing en her kiss

Wherefore ev'ry moment is a little death
Fill'd with indecision, stolen glances,
And a pregnant breath

{**Fingercymbals-Twice**}

An angelic beast born
To the golden bough,

Eye have walk'd amongst the flora and fauna
En search of this strange little girl
With eyes as big as saucers

This strange little girl
(With whom, eye must confess, eye am most enamored)

This strange little girl
This maiden en mourning
This strange snake charmer, silver and
Velvet draped

Whose radiant soul compels her to give
Whilst others (mindful of themselves
                  and their greed only) take

Her splendor?
Her splendor blinds me, brothers

And her fount?
      her fount, extinguishes me, sisters

Dark like clouds
Wet   like rain
She finds me en the thorn bush

Where

Her wine-stained lips lavish my nose with kisses
Aft which

She lowers her head ento the warmth of my mane
And moans,

"So, you have chosen to blister like the Sun,
To fill the ocean floor with monstrous tears
And bear the burden of heartbreak on your knees."

My eyes roll

Eye purr, "*This* is why eye steal stars from the skye.
      This is why water   fills my eyes
      And sorrow my dish.

      A big cat, my love, needs a big fish!"

Nota Bene № 4

In Truth • We Forgot To Clean Our Plates • Started
Coming Home Late • And Took The Rains For Granted •

We Took Ourselves Too Seriously And Stopped Reading
Tuesday's Coffee Grounds • Stopped Being Sweet
To Ourselves And Each Other • Old School I Know •
1st School Fo Sho • We Didn't Feed Love And It Went
Away • And When Love Went Away The Water Went
With It •

A Child Of The Wasteland • A Land Laid Waste •
The Hour Consciousness Fell Upon Me
I Heard The Greybeards Speak Of Water In Abundance •
I Heard Them Speak Of Thales • More Importantly I Heard
The Greybeards Speak Of Origin • Of How The Wasteland
Came To Be •
And It May Surprise You To Learn They Did Not Speak Of
Golden Cups Wounded Kings And Grail Castles • They
Spoke Of Love • That Is To Say • They Spoke Of Love's
Absence And The Grave Consequences That Followed •

- Valentino Santi

Anatomy of A Hero

Nota Bene № 5

Sometimes GOD Is Not Enough • Sometimes Creation
Requires Something More • Especially When The
Winchester Misfires Or The Bolts Of Zeus Scuff Their
Mark • Sometimes FAITH Is Not Enough • Sometimes The
World Is In Need Of More • Especially When Skirts Rise
And Guards Drop • At Which Time The Laundry List
Wears Thin • Rite Ritual Prayer And Sacrifice? • Proper
Tools For A Kingdom Come? • No • I Think Not •

Proper Tackle For A Fisher Of Souls? • Really? •

A Bodhisattva? • A Healer Of Ills? •
Long Shot Ya'll •

Long Shot At Best •
Shot In The Dark At Worst •

And Now •

The Unsavory Rest •

Sometimes The SAINTS Are Not Enough • Sometimes
Life Is In Need Of A Harlot And Sometimes That Harlot Is
In Need Of More Than A Horror Show •
More Than A Catholic Medal Slowly Tarnishing In The
Cleavage Of An Old Woman Or Charms Broken On The
Supple Arms Of Children Who Like To Play With Shiny
Things • Things With Halos • Things With Wings • Things
That Clang And Clatter When The Sarcophagus Door
Slams Shut And The Show However Long Or Short
Arrives At Its End •

- Valentino Santi

The Word

Crackling Meditations by the fyre

Charms of Brass
Charms of Making

Sonnets,
Spells,

Magickal Encantations

Eye believe en paradox
Eye believe en the avarice of language

Meaning

Eye believe The Word is greedy enough
2 take from us
Ev'rything

And generous enough
2 deliver unto the Sons of Adam
A Bettor's Ransom

Eye believe
We need words

Eye believe words possess power
Eye believe (as a Mahogany Angel once said)
They can change the fabric of the World
If and when the Scribbler's pen is endowed w/ purpose

Eye believe words are spears like the Spear of Athena
(Our Lady of Great Wisdom)
Eye believe they can slay Monsters
If and when the Warrior's aim is true

Eye believe
Words need us
And we need (from tyme 2 tyme)
2 draw back the veil

Eye believe words are prescient
Eye believe words are soothsayers

Eye believe they can predict our future
And paint our past w/ firm, broad strokes from a palette
Far more dazzling than anything History can muster

Eye believe words are Sexy

Eye believe they smolder like Hayworth en *Gilda*
Eye believe they tempt the faithful (and rightfully so)
W/ long, black silk gloves and lashes 2 die 4

{Two-Beat Pause}

Eye believe en the power of words
2 seal the present breach
B'tween King, Court, and Providence

Eye believe en their power 2 heal
The 1st wound of Adam's Line

The one they regret
The one they find terribly suspect
The one refusing 2 scab
refusing 2 scar

The one right there
(Self-enflicted)
Above the knee

No . . . not that one
The one right there!

4ever bleeding from the thickest,
Sweetest meat of the thigh

Silly, eye know (maybe it's the demon punch)
But   eye believe a lot of things

Eye believe Sleeping Beauty slept
(W/ one eye open)

Eye believe chocolate kisses keep a girl
Healthy, wealthy, and wise

Eye believe en cities lost beneath the Sea,
Fairy tale endings,
And Golden Asses

Eye believe Ma was right (about James Dean)
Eye believe St. Francis bled thru his robe,
Ruining his tailor-made cuffs
And seams

Eye believe the Tuscan passeggiata
Is a delectable cannibalistic rite 4 the oversexed
And underfed

Eye believe ev'ry outrageous line
Of ev'ry palm ever read

Eye believe The KnightofWands
Is thebestfuckin'card theTarot has2offer aNiggah
En pursuit of answers
En pursuit of aspark

Eye believe chicks w/ pierced lips make the best lovers

Eye believe ev'ry two thousand years a Unicorn
Proclaims the birth of a brown-eyed Mage

And Crystal Skulls are Grigori sent
2 chronicle the present age

{One-Beat Pause}

Eye believe cracks en the wall are genius
And tobacco smoke is good 4 the Soul

Eye believe Mayfield's *Curtis* is a muthafucka!
Grown strong (w/ the death of vinyl)
Not olde

Eye believe Bombshells
Ought 2 be wined, dined, and dipped!

Eye believe Tantric Sex is a means to Salvation
Eye believe the Milky Way is a dish

Best
Served
Cold

And eye believe the splendor of Magdala's supreme claim -

Its pomegranate heart and crack'd alabaster jar
(Tools of the Carpenter's fair Dame)

Is most sacrosanct
    most be-loved

{Two-Beat Pause}

Above all else,
Eye believe words are the earthly agents of the Over-Soul

Alive, they throb
Alive, they save us from darker dayes

Dayes darker than these
Dayes twisted and ill-behaved

Dayes darker than dark
Dayes craved
By Madmen and Miscreants

{One-Beat Pause}

Silly, eye know (maybe, it's the hukkah)

But   eye believe this age is an age
Of undue want and penance

And

The Word,

However it comes ento being,

Will serve 2 free the waters, fill the channels,
And banish it anon

Silly, eye know

But eye believe a lot of things

Nota Bene № 6

Climb Mt. Meru •
Recite *Thunder Perfect Mind* (Mala In Hand) •
Drink Single Malt (Neat) •
Take An Early Morning Train From Roma To Firenze •

We Who Are Apt To Do Such Things
Discovered Early On
That The Hero Is Sometimes Forced Into Glory •
Pushed Out Of The Nest He Stumbles • Pushed Out West
He Is Afraid And Unsure Of His Powers • Unsure He Is
God •

And Like All Conflicted Spiritual Savants Thrown
Bare Knuckled Into This Mortal Coil •
He Seeks Safety •

But Alas The Hero's True Path Does Not Offer Safety •
Neither Cask Nor Comfort Does It Promise •

Verily •
It Promises Sacrifice Only •
The Hero Then
Is A Marked Man •

- Valentino Santi

The Courage of Babylon

Had eye the courage of Babylon
Had eye the mettle to set my Sight above her waist
(Past the beauty mark atop her Righteous shoulder)
The milk of Paradise would not be lost

But alas, eye do not;
And, therefore, can not

Run my Soul aground
When the Black Sea beckons
Its Whyte prow

Wet (w/ rainwater),
She steps from her marble bath
(Rose scented, candle-lit)
Ento an orange Japanese robe

Whose train easily shrouds
The coy inked en the small of her back

A tiffany door ajar,
The lines of her neck
Bring me to my knees

Wherefore the jinn (who conceal my torments daily)
Muffle my screams

When she brandishes a hairpin
And lets down her hair

It is a gorgeous spectacle!
        a prickly harbinger for the gods to weigh

While the throats of their Saints rumble
While the legs of their Statues crumble
While the guardians of their Temples sway

From mare to mare
A prickly harbinger it is!
(Like a suicide of Crows at twilight)

From ley to ley
A gorgeous spectacle it is!
(The gods made to plummet from on high)

{**Two-Beat Pause**}

Her classic silhouette is clearly seen
When she turns her head
And, off the shoulder,
Drops her robe

{**Fingercymbals-Once**}

Had eye the arm of a Giant
(Or the many arms of Vishnu)

Had eye Vulcan's Hammer
   Vulcan's Might

His Farrier's Apron
His Blazing Light

Eye'd strike!
Cold steel
And new shackles forge

But alas, eye do not;
And, therefore, can not

Unbound!
Her lashes caress me
And the candor of her lips hits me hardest
(When wet)

Eye do these things
So you might one daye burn and smell of sandalwood

So you might one daye kiss my breast
And dream such dreams as only cowherders dream
And remember your thralldom crushed underfoot

Unbound!
Her lashes condemn me

To the stones of her scepter
And her Chapel's bitter cup

Unbound!
Her lashes condemn me
To a Promethean trade

Unbound!
Her lashes condemn me
To be free -

An unlikely Hero

Hung

And well made

Nota Bene № 7

Every Goddamn One Of Us
Heard The 1st The Call • And Some • Like The Skunk
Pussies And Dope Fiends Struggled With The Light • We
Discussed It Often • Over Tea • Over Beans On Toast •
We Read It Daily • We Read It In The Post And Dissected
It • BBC4 Reported It • We Watched It And We
Lamented It •

A Stage Theatric • A Poet's Cliché • A Composer's
Leitmotif •
Every Goddamn One Of Us Heard It • We Heard It Loud
And Clear • The 1st Call • That Unremitting Hum
Scratching At The Back Of The Brain •
The Call To The Ignorant • We Heard It Over The Wire •
The Call To The Philistine • We Felt The Nausea • Felt It
In Our Gut • A Thousand Waves Of Sick • A Thousand
Waves Of Wretched Discontent •
This Life This World This Fucking Shit •

- Valentino Santi

Stars & Flowers
(Call to the Philistine)

Stars & flowers
& diamonds & hearts

{One-Beat Pause}

Of me, ask the World
& legions are put asunder

Of me, ask Pow'r
& Kingdoms are cinders
(Left godless en my wake)

Of me, ask Heav'n
& Hades is cast from thine eye

Held captive
By the ripples
Of my waterless lake

{Two-Beat Pause}

There is Sweetness here
& Love (en this simple Call)

Love beyond mere sentiment
          beyond all measure

So,
Of me, ask Love
& my heart, beating w/ abandon,

Is yours

Nota Bene № 8

We Heard It • We Heard Its Prayer Through The Motel
Walls •
We Heard It Yelp • We Heard It Moan • We Heard The 1st
Call •
The Call To The Great Unwashed •
We Heard It And Felt It In Our Bones • Chicken Skin
And Weak Knees •
Every Goddamn One Of Us • We Heard It Loud
And Clear •

Some Did Very Little • Some Did Nothing • Some Did
Dangerous Things • Some Did Too Much •
And Some   .   .   .   Some Slipped Away Quietly Into A
Friary And Some Bought Rifles • And Some Got Drunk
.   .   .   And High •

- Valentino Santi

Tonight

Tonight,
Eye will not take matters
Ento my own hand

Tonight,
Eye will lie w/ her
And listen 2 the band

(Of whyte gold around my finger)

{**Fingercymbals-Twice**}

Tonight,
She will feel me swell enside her

Tonight,
Eye will not be a junkie

Tonight,
Eye will slap her ass
And then,

Perhaps,

Arrive on the slope of her tits

(If the Fallen Nature,
Enside my head,
Allows It)

Nota Bene № 9

Handsome Lad That He Is • He Comes To Us With Lofty
Aspirations •
Ten Legs And Ten Arms Easily At His Disposal •
His Chin Square • His Hair Straight • His Body Strong •

He Prays Nightly And His Spirit Shines Brightly •
He Hears The 1st Call • The Vulgar Call • And Quietly
Discerns Its Every Tremor •
He Reads And Understands Its Every Word And Symbol •
Yet Fails To Act • The Gore Of The TaskAtHand Is Far
Too Much For Him •

A Noble • Aloof By Nature • He Will Not Slum • He Will
Not Stoop •
And From The Skull Of Cain He Will Not Drink
And Be A Bruiser •

O Do Not Judge Him Harshly Folks • Have Pity On Him •
Though His Shoulders Are Broad His Stomach Is Weak
And The Muck Forthcoming Makes Him Queasy •
Yea! He Prays Nightly •

But He Prays For Deliverance Without Trial • Peace
Without Pathos And Balance Without Bloodshed •

A Dragon He Wants To Slay
Without Brandishing Even An Inch of Steel •
Bollocks! •

No Flesh On The Plate • No Bone In The Chipper •
Doesn't Want To Hear Their Ungodly Screams He Says •
Doesn't Want To Rip
And Be A Ripper . . . Doesn't Want To Be A Fool •
Doesn't Want To Be A Fiend •

What He Does Want • In The End •
Is A World Resplendent • A World Redeemed And A
Ledger Kept
Neat And Clean Without The Company Of Odin's Terrible
Horse •

Stupid Kid •

- Valentino Santi

The Great House Speaks

The Great House speaks
And Earth is summoned hastily to bear witness:

From the goatskin of Bacchus,
Eye have tasted my fair share
Of dreams and disappointment

Enough to fill the pockets of ev'ry Sibyl
Enough to know the melancholy of ev'ry Soul,

the crowning fault of Being

Lest eye forget the antiquated poverty
(En this new amoral economy)

The poverty of disparity; to wit,

Light,
Unfettered, blinds the EYE whereas
The Dark, not tempered by the Good, cripples the SEX
Somethin' savage
And severe

Again the Great House speaks
And again Earth is summoned hastily to bear witness:

God of the Trellis
God of the Vine

Let this goatskin pass from me
from this trembling hand
These ashen lips

For eye do not wish to drink
From yur bitter spout
And forsake the stones of my lady's desert tower

Eye do not wish to drink, dream
And be a drunkard

{One-Beat Pause}

A side en this War of Strings,
Eye will not surrender

A side en this War of Maidens,
Eye will not take

> *A poor, lonely boy on a back dirt road,*
> *Eye refuse to load a musket and pierce the wings of my*
> *cousins*

> *Be they Angels / Be they Demons*

> *En twain, eye will not rip their strong shoulders*
> *Eye will not murder their grace*

> *Eye will not bring them to their knees,*
> *Pluck out their spotless eyes*
> *And watch them bleed*

Eye do not wish to drink

When eye can flow
Like a River and be free

Free
Of fallacious encrimination

Free
Of spiritual tyranny

Nor dream

When eye can slip,
Slide, and crash like a Snow-Capped Mountain

From the Crescent
Ento the Sea
Eye wish to stand!
Stand at the Fulcrum,
Seize the Axe
And bring Balance to a Universe paralyzed by poverty

a Universe whose entrails
Are stretched out from end to end

a Universe waiting
For the veins of a Poet, en his prime, to spill pearls
Brash and daring

Pearls worthy of a Black Aethiopian's ear

Eye do not wish
To dream

Eye wish to stand
And take possession of my grandfather's straight razor

Eye wish to stand
And slap it!
Against the ruddy palm of my Sinister hand

Eye wish to hold it,
Stroke it,
And open the width of my veins

Eye do not wish
To be a drunkard

Eye wish
To be a Poet
En his prime

Eye wish
To spill

Nota Bene № 10

Heroes Of A Peculiar Sort • Of A Solitary
Sadistic Purpose •
Of A Single Sick Cloth And Mind •

Usually The One Who Hustles The Seam The Best
Is The One Wounded The Most •
He Sinks The Deepest • He Jumps The Highest • He Runs
The Quickest And Works The Hardest •

He Does The Most Damage • Crashes The Most Cars •
Closes The Most Bars And Bags The Most Bunk • A Pisser
This One Is • A Pisser Fo Sho •

He's A Prophet (When He Walks Into A Room) And Toxic
Because He Spills Frequently
(Into The Palm Of His Righteous Hand) •

A Glorious Vision Of Valhalla In His Eyes (When His
Busy Schedule Allows It) •
Valhalla • It's All About Him • 'Bout His Hate •
'Bout His Fate • 'Bout His Date With A Messianic Destiny
As Yet Unborn •

- Valentino Santi

The Ballad of Jim Jones

Content no longer w/ my lot -
The life of a Man at war w/ himself,
Eye pursued ruthlessly

A god's frock
And cane

And like so many baubles of silver and gold
    like so many   rubies
      so many   pearls
Eye eventually held Light en the palm of my hand

      You should have seen me / Eye was a horny Beast!
            The curl en my hair
           The treachery en my eyes

          Eye heard the Call
          Eye heard it ya'll

          Eye heard it
         And thumped my chest!

          Eye heard it
         And summoned
      Perdition's squires to my stable,
      Its rotting wenches to my fest!

          They fed me
         They clothed me
        They shod my horse

Surcoat
And saddlebags

Silver clamps
Leather straps

{One-Beat Pause}

They armed me
With the rarest of steel

They charmed me
Until the headofmycock got its fill

[A Storm,
Once Menacing And Formidable,
Dissipates
As An American Helicopter Enters Guyanese Aire
Space.

Soon,
Patches Of Blue Appear
And Soon
Skyes Above Waters, Once Turbulent,
Clear.

Squinting,
We Notice A Long, Narrow Footpath Worn
Amidst Acres Of Jungle.

This Worn Footpath, We Follow
(To A Clearing).

This Worn Footpath, We Follow Safely
At A Distance
From Master Bedrooms And Finished Basements.

This Worn Footpath, We Follow,
En Relative Comfort, From Sunken Parlors
And Garage Bars.

This Worn Footpath, We Follow
(To A Clearing).

And Beyond This Clearing,
We Find Gartens Of Collard Greens,
Black-Eyed Peas, And Rice.

And Beyond These Gartens Of Collard Greens,
Black-Eyed Peas, And Rice,
We Find
A Dilapidated Pavilion
And Well.

And Beyond This Well,
Images Of Thatch Huts And Palm Trees Arrive To Us
By Way Of Crack'd Console Television Screens
And Portable Black & Whytes.]

Tho' tremendously flaw'd,
Eye heard it ya'll

Eye heard the Call
Of Stars and Flowers and Diamonds and Hearts
And eye shone en Glory

[Vox Of An Olde Negress Backstage.]
Sho did!

eye shone en Righteousness
Up to my hilt
Thru a dark, dreary Night of
The World's Soul

Eye shone ya'll
Until the coronation en Cali:

Eye kissed the knees of Black Women
And put plastic flowers en their nappy hair

Stoned!
On little whyte pills,
Eye awaited revelation
Behind a pair of dark shades

And those plastic flowers?
Well, they bloomed

And promise,
MY PROMISE,
(So eye thought)
Loomed!

{Fingersnaps-Twice}

Eye shone until ev'rything fell apart

Until the Americas ran out of blessings
And space

Until Jonestown caught fyre (from a sociopathic spark)
And its jungle bled

[We Hear The Chopper's
Propellers Cut The Aire.
We Watch
And Wonder Why The Man Behind The Eyepiece
Doesn't Zoom.

We Wonder . . .
Until He Pans
And Finds His Money Shot.

We Wonder . . .
Until Death Fills The Telly.

Consequently,
We Are Cold And Lonely Around
The Electric Hearth

Until An Unexpected Shiver Breaks The Trauma
And Again We Hear
The Chopper's Propellers Cut The Aire.

En Horror, We Watch
And Wonder Why The Man Behind The Eyepiece
Doesn't Pull Back.

En Horror, We Watch
The Lens Of His Camera Expand And Contract.

We Watch
As It Captures It All / Ev'ry Death Sold,
Dirt Cheap.]

So, the death of my cock
Should not come as a surprise
To anyone

It was not sudden
It did not arrive w/out warning

w/out portents
Tall as a tree, broad as a mountain,
And strong as an ox

[Smiling.]

Lo, the bounty of my work!

Spooks
Po' ass crackas

Goddamn human trash

Dirty, Maoist hippies
W/ Che on the brain

Lo, the bounty of my work!

{One-Beat Pause}

A Deadman's harvest
For the nihilistic soul

Tellin' Niggahs,
Eye hate t' see yo ass leave,
But ya gotta go!

> **[We See Their Lifeless Bodies Face Down**
> **Black, Whyte, And Brown.**
>
> **We See Men Wearing Crosses.**
> **We See Women Clutching Bibles.**
> **We See Children Holding Hands,**
> **Small And Frail.**
>
> **They Wear Sandals, Wife Beaters**
> **And Pleated Pink Skirts.**
>
> **They Hold Dixie Cups**
> **And Vials of Junk.**

Rusted Barrels Of Poison Surround Them . . .
Rusted Barrels Of Flavor-Aid, Ya'll.

Liquid Death 4 The Suckas T' Drink
B'fore Their Memories Shrink
B'fore They Drift
B'fore They Dissolve . . .

Memories Of This Life,
Its Laughter And Love.

{A Loud Handclap - Twice}

Liquid Death 4 The Suckas T' Drink
B'fore They Wise Up
B'fore They Peep The Fatal Hustle
B'fore They Think

On It –

O Dear! O Dear!
The Waste Of It All.]

Nota Bene № 11

What Grit! • And How Unfortunate
For The World •

What Moxie! •
What Huge Fuckin' Balls They Must Have
To Rebuke
A Bringer Of Light In Flight •
And Bruise His Head Beneath Their Heels •

- Valentino Santi

From Parliaments Alien & Strange

From parliaments alien & strange,
A decree of subjugation

Not of our mortal design
Not of our making:

Ento the Pit,
Far from the 7 rivers of Paradise,
Cast him!

Cast him
From thine eye
& bind him to the Rock of Tartarus

There, en that terrible place
They will pain him
They will drain him

They will break his little horn
& bleach his skin
But not claim him

En God's basement, he will linger

Angry & alone

Nota Bene № 12

When The Koi* Speak Of Light • They Do Not Speak Of
The Vulgar Light •
The Light Of Division • The Light Of The World's Ills •
The Light
Of Man's Turmoil • The Light Of Bad Faith •

No •

They Speak Of The Light Of Ages • A Maid Fair Clothed
In The Glory-Of-Elves
Whose Rays Seek To Illumine The Gardens Of God
And Man
And Heal The World's Soul • A Soul Ravaged
By The Vulgar Light •
A Soul Ravaged By Notions Of Love And Truth Poorly
Conceived •

When The Koi* Speak Of Light • They Do Not Speak Of
The Vulgar Light •
They Speak Of The Light Of Ages • A Maid Fair Clothed
In The Glory-Of-Elves •

- Valentino Santi

---

*
Transcended Ones

PARIS

A great many howlers crushed (beneath the wheel)
A great many tumblers tumbling and
A great many Koi troubled by their cyclic charge to find

Yet another Black Dog willing to devour
The heartbreak of Man
And treat the ills of the World

Verily,
They have again chosen well
chosen wisely
(As should you)

After forty dayes and
forty nights
Of peril

They have chosen me
To burn drunkenly
Until the stars of Lyra dim
(Crook en hand)

And be ravishing
And forthright
Until Hera measures thelengthofherhem
And Athena

The lot of
Her whim

{**One-Beat Pause**}

Many elbows kissed
Many opportunities missed

And eye too
(A lowly shepherd / Not yet a dreamer of dayes)
Have chosen

[The Catskills - New York: A Swooping Eagle Cries,
HER HAIR! HER BOSOM! HER BOON!

SHE OFFERS LIGHT! A LIGHT WITHOUT FLAW!
A LIGHT UNMARRED!
A LIGHT BRIGHT AND CLEAR!]

Chosen to swoon
And be swept away
By the rise and fall of a beige French stocking

And touch
Its foam-formed thigh

{Shiver Of A Rattlesnake's Tail}

Aphrodite's cup
Touches my lips

Its rim and stem
She tips

A magnificent act most terrifying
And certainly worth an AppleOfGold

[Mount Ida - Turkey: A Swooping Eagle Cries,
FOR THE FAIREST! THE FAIREST OF ALL!]

Mother of Eros
Mother of Light

Queen of Heaven
Eye am sold

{Two-Beat Pause}

Standing on a mountainside,
By a sacred spring,
Eye flicker with my kinfolk

Verily, eye've chosen well

Mother of Eros
Mother of Light

Banish'd! are my Demons
To catacombs hostile to mortal flight

Cold and silent they lie
On slabs of dank stone
Whereas eye, unencumbered

And sober,

Fly

[Mount Olympus - Macedonia: An Eagle Perched On The
Bough Of A Golden Tree
Sings,
*O! How pleased Ares will be when the Spartans sharpen
Their spears and scale the ramparts of Troy!*

*Kings! Herdsmen! Peasants!
Soothsayers! and Fools!*

Hear this / Know this:

**THE LOGIC IS FUNDAMENTALLY SOUND –
THE HERO, WHETHER LOWLY SHEPHERD OR
DREAMER OF DAYES, IS MET WITH LOVE AND
THE CONTENTS OF HER CUP.**

**EN IGNORANCE, HE DRINKS;
AFTER WHICH THE WAR FOR LIGHT IS
INEVITABLE.**

**A LIGHT WITHOUT FLAW, A LIGHT UNMARRED,
A VIRGIN LIGHT WITH JUICE ENOUGH
TO RESTORE THE KING'S LAND AND SAVE US
ALL.]**

Verily, eye've chosen well
  chosen wisely

To err on the side of Passion
  on the side of Love

{One-Beat Pause}

As should you

Nota Bene № 13

He Will See The Golden Seam Fractured And Choose To
Drop Anchor • No Reason To Believe
He Will Not Loot The Island's Long Forgotten Armory
And Don The Starry Belt Of His Ancestors •

That He Will Eventually Grow Into It And Be The Boxer
We So Selfishly Want Him To Be •
A Boxer Of Mammoth Endurance • A Boxer Of Faith •

A Boxer With A Quick Left Jab And Burly Right Cross •
A Boxer Willing To Take A Sock On The Jaw / All The
While Refusing To Kiss The Canvas Square •

A Boxer Of Extraordinary Albeit Remote Air •
Rightly Disposed To Carry Our Heaviest Loads • Our
Guilt And Transgressions • Our Gluttony And Sloth •

A Boxer Champing At The Bit
To Restore What We Foolishly Tossed Out
Like So Much Goddamn Trash •

- Valentino Santi

Resolution

His Darkness
His Light

His Affliction
His Plight

{Fingercymbals-Twice}

After athousand lifetymes
    athousand Souls spent

Forging Angels' wings
And fixing potholes
(Along dangerous stretches of the King's HWY)

Our workman Mage rises from the stone ruins
Of a once cherished City

{One-Beat Pause}

On the horizon,
He appears

His voice strong
His eyes clear

His code resolute

Without doubt
Without fear

Of the future
Of the loop,

Eye wish U beautiful things, Dearest

This pain shall not prevail
This sickness, eye promise,
Shall not have its way with U

Verily, eye am
Your butter thief

{Fingercymbals-Twice}

Your cowherd with alotmore than alittleFIGHT
Left en 'im

And eye do not entend 2 be the last man standing

{Two-Beat Pause}

Rid of the olde Raiment
the olde Charge

Rid of the olde Earth
the olde War
And all of its accur-sed Lies

Eye entend 2 be a NEW man standing
a NEW man
Most worthy of the boons bestowed upon him by the Stars

Most worthy of the Axe
Most worthy of the Quill
Most worthy of the Lyre

A NEW man,
Eye entend 2 be

With NEW hands
And NEW boots

NEW ships,
Ports, anchors, and lands

{Fingercymbals-Twice}

A man

{One-Beat Pause}

Most worthy of you
Most worthy of your trellis
Most worthy of your bed

And free 2 choose his course

One proper 4 the heart
And the head

Nota Bene № 14

Ankles Ankles Everywhere • But Never A Good Thought
To Think • No Goodness (In This World) •
No Good Deeds (To Find) • No Good Things (To Seek) •

We Wait In Silence • The Snow Falls •
It Falls In The Garden • It Falls In The Street •
But Does Not Stick •
Alas • It Does Not Melt And Give Us What We Need •

We Wait In Silence • A Crow Bleeds • We Wait •
We Toil • We Spin And Woefully Love Does Not Feed •

Calves Calves Everywhere • But Never Hope • Never A
Reason To Believe In The Childhood Promise Of Miss
Thompson's* Knees •

- Valentino Santi

*
Her Beautiful White Legs
No Colorful Tights
No Knee Socks

No, No, No!

Just A Pair Of Big Fat Legs In A Blue Denim Skirt
Beneath A 2nd Grade Desk!

The Champion's Call 2 Arms

One more rabbit hole
One more birth
One more ascension

A new trellis / A new whyte picket fence / Fresh earth

{One-Beat Pause}

One more avatar
One more transformation
One more murder

At the Crossroads

{Fingercymbals-Twice}

Hark!
Love speaks
Love has spoken

Lo!
Love chooses
Love has chosen

From a most unlikely House,
Its Agent

A Bringer of Light
A Bringer of Sight

HIS WORDS!
HIS VOICE!

HIS COUNSEL!
HIS MIGHT!

{Thunderclaps-Once}

The Path Dimly Lit
Unfit 4 Travel

No mule 4 baggage
No shovel 4 shit

Nev'rtheless,
He's needfully drunk (theslaughterofinnocents
                              a mere bump en the road)

Nev'rtheless,
He dances (a somber rogue en new brown skin)

Nev'rtheless,
He's here! (on the case)

{Fingercymbals-Twice}

Here 2 lay siege
Here 2 make things Right!

Hark!
Love speaks
Love has spoken

Lo!
Love chooses
Love has chosen,

From a most unlikely House,
Its Champion

{Two-Beat Pause}

Ghana – West Africa – Dusk.
En A Remote Village,
400 Children Pour From Their Respective Thatch Huts
Ento The Courtyard Of Their Elders.

They Are Naked.
Thin And Strong, Their Brown Bodies Are Painted With
Black Tribal Clay.

They Hold Crudely Constructed Bows.
These Bows, They Feed Equally Crude Arrows.
They Target The Skye. Their Intent?
Strike Angels At Bloody War.
When The Arrows Fly And Disappear Beyond The Clouds,
The Children Shake Tightly Clenched Fists At The Gates
Of Heav'n And Chant,

He's Coming!
He's Coming!

{Two-Beat Pause}

Tanzania – East Africa – Dawn.
En A Remote Village,
400 Children Pour From Their Respective Thatch Huts
Ento The Courtyard Of Their Elders.

They Are Naked.
Thin And Strong, Their Brown Bodies Are Painted With
Whyte Tribal Clay.

They Hold Crudely Constructed Bows.
These Bows, They Feed Equally Crude Arrows.
They Target The Ground Beneath Their Feet. Their Intent?
Strike FallenAngels At Bloody War.
When The Arrows Fly And Disappear Ento The Flora,
The Children Shake Tightly Clenched Fists At The Gates
Of Hell And Chant,

He's Here!
He's Here!

Nota Bene № 15

Eye Am Not This Mudslide • Eye Am Not This Empire
(In Decline) •
Eye Am Not This Suffering • Eye Am Not This Pain •
Eye Am Not This Skin • Eye Am Not This Shame •

Eye Am Not This Mortal Coil • Eye Am Not This Dogma •
Eye Am Not This Name • Eye Am Not This Game •
Eye Am Not This Love •
Eye Am Not Broken • Eye Am Not Disease •

And To
The Delight Of Billions •
My Staff Blooms •

Eye Am Light And Shadow And Change •
Eye Am Being And Non Being •
Eye Am Beyond
The Pillars Of Good And Evil •

Neither Am Eye Nor Am Eye Not •

Eye Am The Well Cover • Eye Cover The Well •
Eye Am This Stream • Eye Am That • And Eye Reference
The God Who May Or May Not Shed Tears
Beneath The Brim Of A Floppy Hat •

Lo!
Eye Am Brahman •

- Valentino Santi

The Soul Factory's Paladin Suite

Cry of the Archer

A Traveler of Worlds
Long b'fore the Castle breach

A Traveler of LightandShadow
Long b'fore the oceans of Gaia dried out

(The Virtues of Water
Ostensibly out of reach)

[A Tiding Of Magpies Caw Aside.]
We shall know him by his scars
We shall know him by his cry

We shall know him by the company he keeps
We shall know him by the keys
to his daddy's car

the car
He wrecks
the car
He drives

We shall know him

know him
By his Karma
know him
By his 3rd Eye.

{Handclaps-Twice}

Long b'fore the silver string of his silver bow is fed
Long b'fore   his quiver is emptied

Long b'fore Boudicca,
With the point of her steel, raps
His wooly head

The Archer's course,

A dissension of nightmares past, present, and future
Takes shape

It is a course of woe
    a course we know
(When we hear his unmistakable cry!)

The course

Of a silverback ape

{Two-Beat Pause}

Friends?
Misplaced loyalty / Misspent youth
And so,
He fails them

Family?
They do not recognise his face
They do not recognise his name
And so,
He fails them

Lovers?
A rude boy
W/ more wit than fame
more bunk than shame

Much too eager to fuck
Much too eager to leave
When the memory of Love's 1st kiss wanes

And so,
He fails them

{Two-Beat Pause}

His need

{One-Beat Pause}

To be loved and adored
Does him en, ya'll

It does him en
Until THE CALL

Of Stars and Flowers
And Diamonds and Hearts

Strikes his Negro brain
W/ a Hammer of Light

{Fingercymbals-Twice}

<u>Rebirth of the Archer</u>

A Dirtworker by nature,
Eye must stop
All this handwringing (and gadding about)
Whenever shit hits the fan

Eye must   .   .   .
ShowMyself greater tenderness
And greater compassion

Eye must   .   .   .
Resist self-loathing
And ev'ry little pinprick
It demands

{Fingercymbals-Twice}

A Lover by trade,
Eye must drink!

      drink
With abandon, from Love's cup
      drink,
With abandon, from Her sweltering Cave

Drink
Eye must

From Her Abundance, Charity
And Grace

{Fingercymbals-Twice}

A Harbinger of Light by default,
Eye must awaken from Vishnu's dream ento mine

Eye must mend
Eye must get well

Eye must
Scar

{Two-Beat Pause}

EyeMust
GetStrong

Strong enough to stitch the hole en my quiver
Strong enough to smith arrows broken
By thoughtless insurrection

By a Darkness (as yet untold)

{One-Beat Pause}

Nev'r mere words
But arrows ancient
    arrows as olde
           as the Gods
Themselves

Perhaps older

Nev'r mere rimes
But arrows sentient

Always cruel (en their honesty)
Always just
Always kind

{Fingercymbals-Twice}

An Archer by necessity
(TheWorldIsNotMine!)

EyeMust
GetStrong

Strong enough to bear
The weight of my bow

And make Right
What the Smoke of 1,200 Gods
MadeWrong

Long ago

{**One-Beat Pause**}

Verily,

Eye must . . .
ShowMyself greater tenderness
And greater compassion

Eye must . . .
Get MyselfTogether

<u>Scar</u>

The Rajah's fast is broken with a question
(Ev'rything is broken with a question)

{One-Beat Pause}

Rajah

Why are my eyes so drawn?
Why am eye not sleeping?

Why do my lips stammer?
Why am eye not well?

{Tabor Drum – Once}

Cowherd

Because
You carry a wound

Rajah

Then why is my armor awash with infirmity?
            my elbows red?
            my waist sticky?

{Tabor Drum – Twice}

Cowherd

Because
You are wounded

{One-Beat Pause}

Tis a mark you bear, Sire
    a mark hidden openly
Atop thy Throne / Beneath thy Crown

    a mark
You do well to hide

            A mark, Sire . . .
        [Thumping His Breast Three Tymes.]
             Enside

Rajah

Ignorant and
Most humble, eye ask

Is it the mark of a crusade
Centuries past?
Or the mark
Of an unreciprocated Love?
Or worse still

A Magician's spell
Meticulously cast?

{One-Beat Pause}

Who or what has wounded me, boy?
Who or what has poison'd my path?

[He Wrings His Hands. He Wrings His Clothes.]

Eye have bled enough t' fill
Athousand oceans and athousand seas!

{One-Beat Pause}

The smell . . .

[En Dismay, He Shakes His Head.]

The smell, Cowherd
Of these blood soaked bandages and the sight
Of these iron stained sheets

Sicken me

Eye'm tired of leaking
          tired of losing strength

          of losing the fight
When the fight is my sacred duty
When the fight is fated to be
          the fightof myLife

Eye am a King en need of Soma, boy
          a King en need of scarring

                    Debt paid
                    Gods appeased

                    Eye've earned
                    A few fucking Scars!

          [Grimacing.]
          Dontcha think?

Cowherd

[Nods En Agreement.]

Eye think .   .   .

It's tyme, Sire
    tyme
To heal
    tyme
To get well
     tyme
To scar

      **[Faces Congregation With Great Poise.
His Mouth Is Serious. His Eyes Are Calm.]**

We cannot
    do   not
Heal w/out scars

There is no healing w/out
        scarring

Scars heal the wound
Scars seal the breach

Scars tell the World we *were* sick
And now we are well

Scars remind us
Of the work (we've put en)

Of our devotion
Of our former shell

Scars remind us
We are better

And have been forgiven
(But not forgotten)

Scars mark the point of entry,
The hour of healing,

And make us feel whole

{One-Beat Pause}

Be not fool'd by the rabble
When they declare, *WE ARE DAMNED!*

Healing is what we do
(When we allow it)

It is what we do
When we end our silence and ask the question

When we sacrifice
Niceties and courtesies
On the altar of dharma

It is what we do
    what we always do
(When we allow it)

{One-Beat Pause}

We heal
We scar
And tell the world
We are better, whole
And free to love

It is what we do
When we enquire

When we ask the King
'Bout his cut

'Bout what ails him

It is what we do
When our query awakens the King
(To the desolation of his Soul /
        the extent   of the damage done)

It is what we do
When the King is fully awake

{**Two-Beat Pause**}

We heal, folks!

We scar

Nota Bene № 16

Enter The Hero • Enter His Horn Of Stars •
His X's And O's •
His Snow White • His Red Rose

Enter The Dancer •
Enter His Black Fedora And Titled Brim •

Enter His Sulphur And Salt And Mercury! •

Enter A Son Of The Auroras • His Arms Raised •
Enter His Niggahs (From The Land Of Khem)
Enter The Sun • Enter The Moon •
Much Older • Much Colder • Much Bolder •

Enter The Hero •
Love's Dusky Champion • The Still Point In His Eyes •

Love's Enemies Defenseless •
Love's Enemies Self-Absorbed •
Love's Enemies Caught By Surprise •

There He Is • Worthless And Nearly Forgotten •
A Fool For The Sake Of Foolishness •

There He Is • A Double Crown Balanced Atop His Wooly
Head • A Black And White Sun •
And By All Accounts Most Unstable And Uncontrollable •
There He Is • A Son Of Hiram •

Enter The Hero •
Enter His Horn Of Stars •

- Valentino Santi

Hubris

I

Ever the Spirit of a decadent Age
Ever the Poet of a land wasted
Drunk and depraved

My greatest rimes are destined to shake
The pillars of God's Kingdom still

My greatest prose
The stars wavering above his head

How long, ya'll?
How long did eye slumber
En the arms of the Bear?

How long has this place been unaware
this place w/out purpose

w/out form
w/out aire?

How long has the WorldofMan
Been a stranger to my face?

How long has this dreary pall
Obscured my race?

My skin like bronze
My limbs like steel

My shoulders like mountains
My eyes like Ezekiel's wheels

Didja miss ya niggah, girl?
Didja think he was dead?

Is that what they toldja?
Is that what you read?

En the tea leaves?
En the coffee grounds?

En the constellations above yur bed?

II

Back from Carthage,
Enside the train's dining car,
Eye open a threadbare curtain

And thru a chipped stained-glass window
Cast my eyes upon orchards unattended
And meadows overrun by the worst vermin

Stiff whyte collars,
They drape their dames en sackcloth
            and their boys en red corsets

While the glory of their noble recitations
 Is awash with blood

Knee deep,
They carry the Holy Writ
They carry the Quran

They carry condemnation
They carry bombs

They carry judgment, brimstone
And cosmic design

They carry a most disquieting paradox
And commit to memory passages from the gospels of
Luke, Mark, and John

And other weak-ass bullshit
Far too vulgar to mention

Back from Carthage,
Eye leave my bags at the station
And enter the city

My guilt razor thin
Slashin' at my ensides

How was eye to know my absence
Would reap a toll as terrifying as this

The King bankrupt
(His Light squandered on a million ruinous things)

His chalice lost
His Queen barren
His river beds dry

A new moon,
He is desperate to shine as he once did
When the Universe was young
And the planets hid from the daughters of men

Back from Carthage,
Eye empty my flask
And smoke my last

Cigarette
(Standing beneath the red and whyte awning
 of the Chelsea Hotel)

Do not retreat
Do not rest

You've come to free the waters,
> *fill our cups,*
> *give us your best*

III

Atop the sheets of an unmade bed,
Eye make my plans
And lay my head

War must be declared!
The waters must be freed
The waters must flow

The King, the Soul,
It has squandered its Light

Balance is lost and
Balance must be restored

My Uncle's pen knife en hand,
Eye carve words ento the hardwoodbody
Of my hotel nightstand

Amid the heather,
Eye will assemble my byrds mountainside

Amid the pine,
Eye will suffer their talons
> *suffer their ridicule*

When eye raise
When eye call

When eye play my hand

Avalanche?
Eye don't think so

Eye will do
All the right things
And make
All the right moves

Steal butter from my Mater's pantry,
Murder a childhood friend

Fuck my twin sister,
Kill my father,
Sire an elephant kin

Swing breathlessly
From the leather bridle of a terrible horse

And drink spiced wine . . .

Of course

{One-Beat Pause}

En tyme, eye will succeed
En tyme, eye will coax Man to challenge the stars

And together we will champion the Soul

The waters must be freed
The waters must flow

Nota Bene № 17

Catapults Strike The Bailey (From The Inside Out) And
They Come • A Soul In Bondage Concedes Its Will To A
Daemon And They Come • A Maid Fair Deep In The Rut
Rakes Her Flesh • She Cries Out
And They Come •

Storm Clouds Gather •
Blood Smeared Thighs In A Bath Drawn Hot Lather
And They Come • The Lies Of The Manor Gain
Momentum • The Lies Of The Manor Shamelessly Step
Into TheLightOfTheSun And They Come •

Bastards • Every Last One Of 'Em • Risen From Ghettos
Like Fiends • Like Black Rats • Like Heroin Crazed
Machines •
Risen From Brothels Cast In Scarlet • Risen From Brothels
Cast In Gold •
Risen From Cracks In Cheap Concrete • A Rose! A Rose!
A Rose! •
Risen From The Tracks Of The French Metro • Risen From
Strasbourg • Risen From Polish Slums •

Spoilt Fuckers! • Every Last One Of 'Em • Risen From
Scottish Rites •
Risen From Polo Fields With Good Russian Ponies
White As Snow And Good Chucks Black As Night •

- Valentino Santi

Scenes from The Wasteland

Nota Bene № 18

In The Days When Darkness Prevailed • The Moon
Did Not Give Her Light •
Steadfast • She Did Not Reflect The Golden Rays
Of Her Brother And Consort •
Hence The Great Gift Of Prometheus • The Gift For Which
He Suffered And Paid So Dearly • Fell Into Disrepair And
Out Of Favor •
The Great Gift Of The Titan • Molder Of Clay •
Bringer Of Light • Bringer Of Sight •

Verily •
Forethought Gave Way To Survival
As Thorns And Thistles Choked The Garden
And Paranoia Filled Mortal Lungs •

Verily •
We Were Anxious • Anxious About Drying Oceans •
Anxious About School Shootings •
Anxious About The Bodies Of Young Boys Found
Beneath Floor Boards •
Anxious About Oil Drums And Fuel Injections • Anxious
About Bar Codes • Anxious About Grimy Truck Stops And
Greasy Spoons • Downloads And Prepubescent Thongs •

We Were Terrified • Terrified By What We Had Become •
By The Shoes We Chose To Wear And The Shit
We Chose To Spew •
Atop Shadowy Mountains • In Thick Poisonous Air •

And So • We Panicked •

We Flogged Our Soothsayers •
We Tortured Our Magicians • We Sent The Holy See
Into The Bush With Very Explicit Orders •

Burn The Devil's Cards • Break His Bones •
Deface His Runes •
And Fell Every Goddamn Tree In His Worship •

Yet •

SHE Remained •
In Spite Of Our Thorough Cleansing •
In Spite Of Our Atrocities • Our Trains •
Our Showers • Our Ovens •

A Broken Beacon She Nevertheless Stood •
Not Quite The Moon •
Not Quite A Reflection Of The Sun's Golden Rays •
Not Quite The Boon Of Prometheus • But True •

True Enough To Be Seen Through The Madness •
True Enough To Be Heard Above The Ruckus •

- Valentino Santi

Zelda, A Sibyl Disjointed

I

Courtesy o'er
Cocktails and
Cocaine

They said so many things (o'er all those miserable years)
Some to my liking and some . . . **[Grimacing.]**
Not so much

They said eye was drum
And cymbal

They said eye was Zeitgeist,
A Spirit of the Age!

{One-Beat Pause}

They said eye was glorious,
The New Eve

Nobrain and
Allknees

They said eye was Golden

A daughter of the South,
Pride of the bars and stars

{Fingercymbals-Twice}

They said eye was eccentric, erratic,
A lass unbelievably lush

Ev'ry Mother's cornfed nightmare
Ev'ry Schoolboy's 1st
Shithouse crush

Then . . . after too many dark dayes
(Each
Darker than the next)

They said,

The poor girl is breaking
The poor girl is broken

This, we say / See her sway?
Bad wiring en the way

Finally!
The Sportin' Life has caught up to her
And made a dent

The flaw en the design
Those lapses / That rent

It is all too much
For our shoulders to bear

[A Mere Afterthought.] *And hers*

HEY, MINI! HEY, TONY!
YA DON'T KNOW YUR ONIONS

SHE'S SICK, EYE TELLYA, STANDIN' HERE OV'R THE
BATHROOM SINK

AND SOMEBODY'S GOTTA HOLD
HER FUCKING HAIR!

[Niggers Aside.]
We'll do it!
We'll bind 'er

We'll bind 'er pretty whyte feet
And pretty whyte hands

We'll do it, Mistah Charlie!
We'll bind 'er

We'll bind Zelda -
It's for 'er own good
Ya know .   .   .

II

The Spiders meet en the upper room
And exchange pleasantries

They count their crucibles,
Nod their heads,

Grunt,
And peruse their dog-eared books

Cordial fuckers!

{Two-Beat Pause}

Those studious frocks
And argyle socks
Don't fool this belle

They look like pimps

[Spiders Aside.]
Here is a Woman stricken
A Woman ashen

Drowning en the depths of hysteria

Now weak
Now strong

When and where the mood strikes her
Whether or not
She is Right or Wrong.

{Fingercymbals-Twice}

They scratch their grey chins,
Initial, en blue ink, the necessary papers,
And shoot Francis, from ev'ry possible angle,
Athousand disheartening looks

After a while,
The Housekeeper packs Zelda's bags

After a while,
Scottie's eyes fill with water

After a while,
A long black car arrives
And kicks up dust

Whereby
Zelda is Nowhere

Whereby
Zelda is Here

{One-Beat Pause}

And her haunts
Are the haunts of athousand unspeakable things
And all the great Evil they bring

Evil unbound

Evil tempered
Neither by Grace
Nor   by what is Good and Just

{One-Beat Pause}

Alas! Zelda is Here,
Entombed en Herself

Her bath,
A bath drawn
From the lather of horses,

Nightmares nev'r sated
But hidden away

Messily,
Eye'm afraid to say,
En crawl spaces fit for a Frankish King
(Who just happens to prefer the company of butchers)

[Spiders Aside.]
They are Metaphors!

Metaphors
For a Madness once loosed
Now kept.

{One-Beat Pause}

Alas! Zelda is Here
En the garten of her Lord
En the garten of her Fathers
En the garten of her Faith

And her deliriums
Are hers and hers alone

[Spiders Aside.]
Inventions of loneliness
Inventions of torture
(Not to mention
All those wicked sins).

{Fingercymbals-Twice}

Alas! Zelda is Here
Where no opium dream (of which to speak)
      no literary wonder, with a needle en his arm
Or tumbler on hand

Is found
And bought
Dirt cheap

{One-Beat Pause}

Alas! Zelda is Here
When more Christ Killers come
With their flip charts, leaky fountain pens,
Shy locks and walls of olde world sheepskin

Alas! Our heroine is Here
When the Spiders direct the Niggers to hold her down
So they can stick her with their long knives
And   fill her gut
With pills

[Zelda Aside.]
It is a daily struggle
To walk these floors and conjure words.

My legs are flabby (from the hospital junk) . . .
My thoughts a mess.

Francis,
Eye am a goddamn sight.

Her skin bubbles,
Bleeds and burns

[Zelda Aside.]
There is poison on my skin
And acid beneath my tongue.

And they tell her
She is gone

   . . . allgone
Nothing left

A no-thing
A non-soul

[Niggers' Jungle Chant Aside.]
Anātman!
Anātman!
Anātman!

{A Hindu Drum Rattle Shivers Softly To Fade}

Her beautiful glass slipper
Falls ento the hands of a notorious Yankee Queen
(Or so they tell me)

   . . . but of *this*
Eye am certain

{Fingercymbals-Twice}

Rid of his Irish pluck
Rid of Doughboy summers on the Riviera
Rid of carriage rides en the park

Rid of The Vanderbilts
Rid of Negroes en Harlem after dark
(All tails and top hats)

Rid of Ernest
Rid of Clara's pout
And red flair

Rid of Coco's chic, her Ready-To-Wear,
And Louise's cold,
Black helmet hair

{Two-Beat Pause}

Francis,
Aptly attired,
Will visit

He will wear his wrinkled blue suit,
A stained tie and a pair of Italian leather shoes
(Borrow'd *and* Scuff'd)

Reeking of Boston gin,
He will steady a broom and dust pan
And sweep the hospital floor

He will ignore my cries,
Reeling from his lies,
And painstakingly sift thru athousand cones of ash

He will steal the meat of my misery
And leave the fat

Dotingly,
He will look upon my face

Post Helen
Post Troy

And give my crown a pat

Eye'm tender-headed!
Eye'll remind him
Don't you remember?

III

If we are here (and we are)
Then surely we were built for these dark,
Difficult dayes

Forged en their likeness,
Surely we share their pluck, shimmy
And shake

So, it is most curious
The choices we make

{One-Beat Pause}

We choose want
When the pantry latch is broken

[Aside.]
Butter 4 Ev'ryone!
Butter 4 AAAALLLL those
Hyperborean folk who readily heed
The grey cloud elephant's unearthly call.

So, it is our lot

{Fingercymbals-Twice}

We choose brutality
When beauty stands dripping wet on our stoop
And seductively beckons,

Water passes from me, anon
Eye bid thee – DRINK!
Drink and be free
Drink and be me

So, it is

We choose fear
When love is clearly due

What is worse

En the sick glow of Man's little
Misanthropic enterprise

We fear Life (if you can believe that shit)
And   Death

{One-Beat Pause}

And all
The biological *bull*shit that lies en between

It's all the same   .   .   .   *we're*
      all the same

[**Aside.**]
Spoilt little fuckers!

Too stupid and
Too slow-witted
To see the Light

En need of wisdom
En need of grits and greens

En need of a firm Confederate handshake
En need of a goddamned switch.

IV

We hate it
We hate this

{One-Beat Pause}

We hate
Ev'ry stinking moment
(Of our stinking lives)

We hate ev'ry radio knob and movie screen
We hate ev'ry flapper
Wise (beyond her years)
En ev'ry pulp magazine

We hate it
We hate this

We hate being this way
We hate being askew

Ev'ry jagged ascent
Ev'ry   swoon
Seemingly benign

{One-Beat Pause}

We hate the crash (when it fucking comes)
And the subsequent knowing . . .

That we are pain junkies still
Strung out on the filthiest of thrills
And their devices of unimaginable degradation,
Wealth, and fame

All this,
Shug

Tho' we keep our eyes
On ev'ry rainbow en ev'ry skye

{Two-Beat Pause}

That said

We hate it!
We hate this

{Two-Beat Pause}

Behold!

Where mighty lakes once stood,
En the garten of our Lord
En the garten of our Fathers
En the garten of our Faith

Dry beds of rocky, barren soil
Now stand

{One-Beat Pause}

They told us

The grass is always greener
This side of Paradise

Isn't that what he said?
Isn't that what he

[Confused and Embarrassed.] um . . . they
Told us?

The grass is greener
The Niggers meaner

[Niggers Aside.]
Hey! Their lips are bigger (and so)
The wine is sweeter.

{Two-Beat Pause}

If that's so,
What's all this then?

Prêt-à-porter!

{Fingercymbals-Twice}

Ready-To-Wear people living
Ready-To-Wear lives

Populated by
Ready-To-Wear pool parties, stag-flicks,
And long, winding, blacktop drives

With their

Ready-To-Wear daisies and
Ready-To-Wear lawns

[A Schizophrenic Aside By Zelda.]
Who are these miserable fucks?

[Now Softly, Another Schizophrenic Aside By Zelda.]
You'll know them   .   .   .
By the cut of their jib.

They are
What they are.

{Fingercymbals-Twice}

Namely,

Ready-To-Wear dolls
Bound by the collar
And cross

To

Ready-To-Wear fools

Who nev'r miss an opportunity
To froth at the mouth, hiss, and drool

{A Single Heavy Sigh}

Quiet as it is kept,
There is shit, knee-deep,
This side of Paradise

Eye don't care what he said
Lies! All lies

Eye don't care what he
[**Confused.**] *Goddamnit!*
  . . . they
Told us

This is no good

Love has gone out of the World

V

Soon,
Death will call upon me
(As eye lie here);
But eye am not afraid, Mama

Past iron gates
Past barred windows

Past watchmen en cheap black boots
And starched whyte shirts

Past heavily chained six foot doors
Past wooden fyre escapes

Death will make her way,
Unseen, to the kitchen

She will make her way
And eye will, no doubt,
Hear her tongues split the galley floor

And rattle a cage
Of pots and pans

{One-Beat Pause}

Soon,
Death will call upon me

She will blister thru the dumbwaiter
She will blister thru the roof

She will blister thru ev'ry antiseptic hall, pantry
And hospital door

And soon,
Very soon,

She will stand at the foot of my bed
With a flask of whiskey in her coat pocket

Alas, she will get me drunk, get enside my head,
And fuck me with her fabled schoolyard charms

And

After a brief courtship,
Her tongues will rake my flesh and
Make me a docile Lover

A Lover en decline
A Lover en peril
A Lover en an awful state

Ready to break the shackles of the Living
And go home

So,
Eye will lie here

Aware of my bruises
Aware of my fate

And soon,
My lungs will fill with black smoke
My brain   with pins
And needles

Eye will writhe and
Eye will smell burning flesh; but,

EYE

WILL

NOT

STIR

Eye will lie here
And await her kiss

Eye will lie here
And await her final push
Ento my soul

Eye will lie here
And await the end of all burdens
            the end of all sorrows
            the end of all pain

Eye will lie here
And await

A pilgrim's journey home

{Two-Beat Pause}

Here!
A gift for you, Shug

The mortal remains of a Sibyl, disjointed
                              a charred body

Of burnt hair and bones
Once easily broken

{One-Beat Pause}

Eye am gossamer now . . .
Barely anything at all

A solemn wraith
Beyond the reach of flesh and bone

Fated to negotiate the olde ford,

That dreadful place
Where Life and Death meet
And exchange looks of longing

Where ev'rything, eye am told,
Comes to a boil

VI
Conclusion: A Disjointed Sybil's Prayer 4 The Wasteland

We are sovereigns, you and eye
          sovereigns
Detached from the Real

{Two-Beat Pause}

The evidence of this truth
Is as terrifying as it is obvious

War, Poverty, Thralldom!

Alas,
We can no longer afford to work and play
En the World of Abstraction

    the World of I-dea, Hope
And Promise
When these dark, difficult dayes demand much more

{One-Beat Pause}

We

Must *be* more!

We must engage
And make our presence known
Enside the Ring

THIS IS NOT A PRIVATE FIGHT!

It is a public brawl,
Bloody and without regret

Note well, Shug
The sign posted above the Coliseum arch

**KINGS AND QUEENS
ARE MOST WELCOME**

Nota Bene № 19

We Found Pages Of His Book • The Book Of Travis •
A Book Of Canticles •
We Found Pages • We Found Fragments •
Fragments In Various Stages Of Decay • We Found Pages
Of His Thimk Book •
We Found Them Amongst The Glass And Steel Ruins Of
His Fabled Island City •

The City He Roamed •
The City He Inadvertently Flooded •

No One Believed • No One Believed
The Tulane Expedition • No One
Believed The Word When The Word Got Out •
Isn't He An Old Wives' Tale? They Said •
Isn't The Diary A Matter Of Fiction? They Cried •
No One • No One Believed The Word
When The Word Got Out •

They Believe It Now Though • They've Read The
Fragments • They've Seen The Bullet Holes • They've
Tasted The Blood • They've Waded Through The Garbage
• They've Waded Through The Shit • They've Waded
Through The Flood •

They've Digested Each And Every Line •

A Pusher • They Believe In Him Now •
A Preacher • They Believe In The Rain • A Strong Rain •
A Heavy Rain •
A Real Rain • The Rain He Saw Clearly In His Head •

A Rain That Fell • A Rain That Washed Away The Filth •
A Rain That Washed Away The Scum • A Rain That Fell
On The Righteous And UnRighteous Alike •

It Fell In Buckets • And Irises Flourished •
They Flourished Far From The Island City • Far From Its
Ticket Diners • Far
From Its Halls Of Fascination • Its Halls Of Iniquity •

Far From The Wizard's Skull Cap
And Crystal Ball •

We Found Canticles Ya'll • We Found Pages
Of His Book • We Found Fragments •

We Found The Book
Of Travis •

- Valentino Santi

Memories & Dreams

Phragment 1

Tho' he is a shadow amongst shadows
(Lepers, Junkies, and Scoundrels!)
A Man may reinvent himself
(And, from tyme to tyme, refashion reality to his liking)

Seeking momentary solace
En the slip of a whyte girl's kiss,
He may purge the Creator's Human Design
Of its obligatory flaws! Cruelty, Desolation, and Guilt

A Pilgrim on the mend, he may fell mountains
If they hinder his turn thru the wood,

E-A-T the clouds if they happen to bleed darkness
Ento the skye, or clothe the rays of Apollo
                    if they wither his garten

A Knight of Faith
A Knight of Love

He may lay waste to the World
(Stem t' stern)

If It displeases him greatly
If It does not share his appreciation
For Ms. Dorothiea H. Patton
Or bend to his Will

If It does not panic at the peculiar shape of his Wings
Or lean on his throne
The 1st daye of Spring

Shivering to the marrow
Shaking to the bone

{**One-Beat Pause**}

If It does not strive toward
What He knows en his Heart to be Right and True; namely,
The Highest Good

[**Aside.**]
Whatever that is.

Nota Bene № 20

In The Days Of Blood And Sand •
Days Of Thirst • Days Of Hunger • Days Of Woman •
Days Of Man •

We Were Always
Elbow Deep In Shit •

More! More! More!

More Junk • More Flesh • More Gold •
More Cedar • More Funk • More Garters • More Pussy •

More! More! More!

More Until There Isn't Anything Left •
More
Until The Masses Are Bereft Of Soul •
More
Until The Everyday Grows Tired
And Old •

- Valentino Santi

Phragment 2

Here eye stand on the crag of enlightenment,
My lips wet with soma
My Right shoulder burdened with Anxieties
My Left with unconquerable Fears

{Two-Beat Pause}

From the ashes of a ground burning,
Questions arise and sear my brain:

Atop Mt. Moriah
W/ dagger en hand

Atop Mt. Moriah,
Observing the threshing floor
Of Adonai's desert
    Adonai's barren land,

Will Faith become me?

Will it rip me to pieces
When the blood of Isaak
Brims God's cup?

Nota Bene № 21

The Impersonal Does Not Always Serve Our Thing Well •
It Does Not Strike The Heart • Does Not Wreck The Soul •

It Does Not Leave Us Gasping •
Gasping For Air • Gasping On The Floor •

It Does Not Leave Us Shattered •

Indeed • We Need Not Only What Is Buried
(Just Beneath The Skin) •
We Need The Personal • The Intimate •

We Need Pleasure • We Need Pain •
We Need What Is On The Surface • We Need What Rises •
We Need The Cream •

Let's Face It • We NEED The Skin •
What Is Easily Forgiven But Rarely Forgotten •

- Valentino Santi

Phragment 3

Awake, he lies en a garten of olde friends -
Bones buried beneath the moon and stars
Bones buried en the snow
Bones . . . awaiting resurrection
                awaiting
Some strange herder's call

Awake, he lies
And fondly thinks of a girl from athousand fares gone by
                a girl who was once his pearl

He remembers the smell of her cherry red hair
And her breath, hot and sweet, against his neck

Waves, rapturous and relentless, batter him!
The Righteous corner of his mouth quivers whilst
The butterflies en his stomach pinch his liver

Awake, he lies
And tries to remember
The first tyme he held her hand en his
The first tyme his lips touched the back of her knees
The first tyme he pressed a blue iris petal against her cheek

Nota Bene № 22

Keep Moving •
Lest You Stop Long Enough To Catch Your Breath •
Lest You Stop Long Enough To Hear The Poet's Lyre
And Read His Runes •

Hold Steady •
Lest You Learn The Bitter Truth • Lest You Learn That
LOVE Has Flown •
Lest You Drag The River • Lest You Find His Head •
Lest You Hustle • Lest You Ask Those Questions
Reserved For The Rishi At Heart •

Questions Reserved For The Seekers •
Reserved For The Sowers •

Hold Steady • Hold Steady Boy •
Lest His Call Rattles You •
Lest It Stirs You From Safety •
Lest It Stirs You From Your Deepest Sleep •

- Valentino Santi

Phragment 4

Lo! The birth of a Lyon
(The truest measure of an Age)

Behold! His Mohawk stride
Marvel! Murderer! Mage!

{Two-Beat Pause}

.   .   .   Heav'n *and* Hell
Have suffer'd shipwreck

Enter a Miracle w/ fresh vines -
Words beautiful, bold and fine

Come! Witness
The birth of this new Hektōr

[A Dusky Daughter Of Mars Aside.]
What ya see
Is what we got.

{A Cowbell-Twice}

A Man   .   .   .

Who will not take it anymore
Who will not give ground (to the road beneath his cab)
Who will not give quarter

Who will not raise the whyte flag
For the dopers to see
(And take comfort as a result)

Nota Bene № 23

Life In The City Is Quite Unforgiving •
It Is Cold And Rotten •
A Cesspool In Which Great Men Are Often Reduced To
Wretched Creatures • Beasties Forlorn And Forsaken •
A Cesspool In Which Common Men Spit Curses And Ask
Curious Questions Again And Again •

Where O Where Has God Gone?
Where O Where Are His Angels And Saints?
His Pillars Of Smoke?
His Palaces Of Light?

Great Men And Common Men Alike
Shake Their Tightly Clenched Fists
At The Gates Of Heaven •

They Burn Torches • They Hold Pitch Forks High •
They Storm The Grounds And Ask Curious Questions
Again And Again •

Why Does He Not Fix Every Goddamn Thing
When He Knows We Have It Hard?

Why Does He Not Summon The Rains
When He Knows We Have Played Our Last Hand,
Turned Our Last Trick,
Smoked Our Last Joint, And Made Our Last Stand?

- Valentino Santi

Phragment 5

The Voices
Are relentless

They do not wane
They do not rest

They will not grant
A niggah peace

[The Voices Aside.]
You are a dead Man wearing
A drinking Man's yoke.

[Shaking Their Heads.]
Tsk. Tsk. Tsk.

Too fuckin' easy . . .
A maritime gorilla
Ripe for the picking.

{Fingercymbals-Twice}

Alien, is he still,
To the thumb-sized Heart
Of a frail, little boy he once knew well

Whose greatest wish
Echoes anon,

RICH! RICHER! RICHEST!

Nota Bene № 24

No Moon • No Stars •
No Death • No Life •

The Ego Has Doomed Us All • It Wants
Too Much (From A World Driven By Will) •
It Wants Happiness Without Sorrow • It Wants Love
Without Heartbreak •

The Ego •

It Has Doomed Us • It Has Broken Everything •
It Has Smashed Bliss Into A Thousand Cruel Pieces •

And Consequently •
Things Are Not As They Should Be •
Not As They Need To Be • Not As They Once Were •
Not As They Can Be •

Yes • The Ego Desires •
But It Is Mostly A Lopsided Affair •
It Desires Balance On Its Own Terms • A Selfish Balance
That • If Rumors Are True Does Not Care Much
For Shiva's Dance • For Cows And Elephant Caves •
For Sacred Ritual And Drunken Romance •

- Valentino Santi

Phragment 6

Enspite of ev'ry dreadful thing
Enspite of Hindoo mantras

Sung
Off –key

Enspite of Betsy's betrayal

Enspite of sorrow
Enspite of selfishness

Enspite of rancid pulp,
Barren seeds, and
A soft rind

Enspite of loneliness

Enspite of non-being
Enspite of being   .   .   .

Lonesome

{One-Beat Pause}

Eye gotta do somethin' and
Eye gotta do it now

Some way
Some how

.   .   .   DAMN!

Nota Bene № 25

The Watchers Foretold These Days
With Great Trepidation • Days Of Cowardice • Days Of
Fear • Days Of Lives Poorly Lived •
Lives Counterfeit And Soulless •

The Lives Of Ghouls •

Ghouls Who Break Bread
But Do Not Eat • Who Track Game But Do Not Cut
The Fat From The Meat •

Discrimination It Seems Has Gone Out Of The World • Its
Powers Have Diminished • Folks Can't Tell Good Apples
From Bad • Can't Tell Love From Apathy • Happy Faces
From Sad • Saint From Scum •

- Valentino Santi

Phragment 7

We claw
And tear

Eyes and hair

(When the beast grows
Too big for the well)

WAR! eye have declared it .   .   .   and
At long last
WAR! has found me

Free

Free from the sewers
Free from the shit .   .   .

Nota Bene № 26

WE
Are Ghouls And
WE
Are In An Awful State •

Alas • We Sit And Do Nothing •
We Stand And Do Nothing •
We Sleep And Do Nothing • We Labor And Do Nothing •

Dig This • Paris Burns • Roma Crumbles • Firenze Slips
Quietly Into The Sea • And Nothing Happens • Nothing
Gets Right • Nothing Gets Polished • Nothing Gets Done •

- Valentino Santi

Phragment 8

All this darkness
All this heat

All this rage
All these troubling visions (on the mystic's page)

All this wisdom (clearly and beautifully revealed)
All these

{A Heavy Sigh}

Fantastic dreams at night

All this pow'r
All these words misspelled, misunderstood,
And misguided

All this goddamn fear
All this might .   .   . has to go

Somewhere

{Two-Beat Pause}

Right?

{Fingercymbals-Twice}

Nota Bene № 27

Men Of Letters • Men Of Knowledge • Renowned Men •
The Philosopher • The Mountebank • And Even The
Theologian Arrived Too Late To The Ball • Too Late To
Ponder The Enormous Weight Of It All •

The Weight Of It •
When The Oceans And Rivers Dried Up •

The Weight Of It •
When The Number Of Grazing Cattle Thinned And Every
Crop In Every Field Turned To Dust •

The Weight Of It •
When Everything Went Wrong •
When Everything High And Low Began To Rot •

The Weight Of It •
When Love Became A Dirty Word •
A Filthy Little Thing • A Slimy Sewer Bomb •

- Valentino Santi

The Apologia of King David

Thru his junkie shoulder,
Clear to the bone,
The scars of Hell
The scars of penance are thoroughly

And

Regrettably

Sown

[Aside.]
When Roe hears those dark, narrow shoulders creak -
Woefully, she moans.

{Handclaps-Twice}

On the hip
His nose drips
(Minor chords fill his brain)

It gives him strength
(This shit en his veins)

It gives him the courage to sit
On his Mama's piano bench,
Feel the keys, once more, beneath his fingertips
And sing his much heralded lament

The lament of a junkie
The lament of a Life poised

To grind his Soul ento powder,

Dig a hole
And bury

Whatever remains

The Lament

A predicament fo sho

Body's breakin' down
Werks ain't no good

Can't find a decent vein
And Mama's olde house spoon
Don't cook junk like it should

And sometymes the needle cuts flesh
And eye bleed on the flo

Sometymes eye bleed on my shoes
And sometymes eye bleed on my shirt

Eye bleed until eye'm sick
Eye bleed until eye'm tired

{One-Beat Pause}

Tired of bein' barren
Tired of lungs black as coal
And skin black as tar

Tired of hatin' Crackas
And Jews
(4 all their worth / 4 what they are)

Tired of long knives
Splittin' a Niggah en two

Tired of hatin' m'self

Tired of muthafuckas (a lot like you!)
Puttin' Love on the shelf

When it's Love that drives ev'rything

{Two-Beat Pause}

When it's Love that drives us all

Nota Bene № 28

It Was Always There • Just Beyond Our Reach • Just
Beyond The Fullness Of Our Understanding • Outside
It Stood • Outside It Took Root • Outside Our Marginal
Vision •
Somewhere • Out There • Over The Hills And Past
The Railroad Tracks • Near The Sacred Trellis Where
Every Mystery Is Made Known
To Those Who Seek Them With A Good And Tenacious
Heart •
Outside It Stood • Something Unthinkable • Something
Utterly Impossible •

No Matter How Hard We Tried To Imagine It
And Make It Real • Real To The Eye •
Real To The Touch • Real To The Tongue • Real To The
Teeth • No Matter How Hard We Tried To Conquer
The Fear Of It •
And All The Monsters That Came When It Beckoned •
No Matter How Hard We Tried To Rebuke The Sex Of It •
Straight And Rigid • No Matter How Hard We Tried To
Wash Away The Stench Of It •

It Was Always There • Just Beyond Our Reach • Just
Beyond The Fullness Of Our Understanding • Beneath The
Shade It Stood • On A Precipice •
Near The Sacred Wine Press • Near The Sacred Wood •
Ever Eager To Reveal Itself To A World
Short On Goodness • Short On Tenacity • Yet Long On
Hate • Long On Violence • And Long On Dark Days •

There It Stood • And We Were To Blame •
There It Stood • And We Were Ashamed
When Rigor Set In • There It Stood
And There It Came • The Death Of Every Decent Thing •
Every Bottle Of Single Malt • Every Beautiful Woman •
Every Diamond Ring •

There It Stood • King Of All Fears •
There It Stood • After One Too Few Beers •

There It Stood In Vicksburg • There It Stood In Taipei •
There It Stood In Berlin • There It Stood In Marseille •
There It Stood In Rome •

The Death Of Love •

There It Stood • At The Hearth •
There It Stood • At Home •

- Valentino Santi

Eulogy

**[The Honorable Pastor Danville,
Immaculately Dressed En A Black Roman Cassock
With Red Trim, Steps To His Oak Pulpit.
His Negro Congregation Is Silent When He Catches The
Eye Of His Most Trusted Deacon, Straightens His
Cassock's Shoulder Cape And Begins,
En Ernest, His Sunday Sermon.]**

If ya'll came here
Half-expectin' me t' heap undue praise upon Brother Love
Ya'll gone leave God's House
With a sad and heavy heart

If ya'll came here
Half-expectin' me t' play it safe
               t' seize the middle
               t' be coy
And dodge the dark patches of his all-too-brief Life
Ya'll gone leave God's House
With a sad and heavy heart

If ya'll came here
Half-expectin me t' **NOT** froth
               t' **NOT** holla from the Cave of my Soul
               t' **NOT** crawl along the Jordan's edge

For a drink from his robe
    a drink from his bowl

Ya'll gone leave God's House
With a sad and heavy heart

If ya'll came here
Half-expectin' me t' **NOT** call him *MyNiggah*
　　　　　　　　t' **NOT** holla the Truth and Tragedy
Of Brother Love
Ya'll gone leave God's House
With a sad and heavy heart

If ya'll came here
Half-expectin' some supreme Act of Contrition
　　　　　　　some supreme Act of Gravity-Defying Will
Ya'll gone leave God's House
With a sad and heavy heart

'Cause we ain't got tyme for that

These dayes are short, Brothas!
Too short for Crenshaw County
Too short for pecan trees

These dayes are short, Sistahs!
Too short for juke joints
Too short for country grammar
And smokin' weed

[Negro Congregation.]
Yes, Lord.

So

If ya'll came here
Half-expectin' me t' sing and pray
And mop my brow with Orgia's handkerchief

{One-Beat Pause}

If ya'll came here
Half-expectin' me t' wield one of Bera's homemade fans

Ya'll gone leave God's House
With a sad and heavy heart

[Pastor Danville, On The Verge, Sips Clear Shine
From The Mason Jar Ever Poised Atop His Pulpit
And Smacks Clean His Thick Blue Lips.
His Voice Now Fill'd With Brimstone,
Pastor Danville Resumes His Sunday Sermon.]

Now!

If ya'll came here
Half-expectin' me t' set it off
Half-expectin' me t' set it straight
Ya'll gone be all right

Ya'll

{Two-Beat Pause}

Gone be
All right

**[Pastor Danville Holds Up High
A Weather-Worn Copy Of** *The Herder's Tome.*
**He Then Slams The Book Atop His Pulpit,
Opens It And Reads,
With His Usual Fury,** *An Ode 2 Love.***]**

Here!
Here lies the fallen sandal tree
Here lies the perfumed axe

Here lies the city of Jerusalem en ruin

Its burning orchards and
Crumbling stone

Here!
Here lies the Skins of Tyme
And the memory of Waters
From them drawn

Behold! The Franciscan meal

Not whatcha think
But whatcha truly feel

[Pastor Danville's Negro Congregation En Unison.]
Yes, Lord.

Here!
Here **HE** lies

Lord of Lords
King of Kings
Sage of Sages

A butter thief
A note unstruck

{The Force And Weight Of Pastor Danville's Black Blue Fist Atop His Pulpit}

A ROCK OF AGES!

{Two-Beat Pause}

A Supreme Ruler
A Supreme Charioteer

Who once drove Ev'rything
Who once drove us ALL

Until **WE**
Drove **HIM**
Away

{Fingercymbals-Twice}

O The Tragedy of Love!
Man's most diabolical handiwork
    his most
Unforgivable trespass

    his latest and
Greatest failure -

An homage to atrocity

O The Tragedy of Love!

[Pastor Danville, En Need Of A Respite, Again Sips Clear Shine From The Mason Jar Ever Poised Atop His Pulpit. Consequently, As The Brimstone Is Shaken From His Black Blue Throat, His Voice Grows Soft And Solemn En Tone.]

When we thirst'd,
He gave us drink

When our bellies growl'd,
He gave us parchment
Gave us ink

And

When we were wayward, lost en the dark wood,
He shone brightly en the night like the flicker of a diamond
On a Magdalene's wrist

{Two-Beat Pause}

When we fell ento the tar pit,
He drew a Roman bath

When we dripped decadence,
He washed behind our ears

Between our fingers
Between our toes

And

When, en the depths of our Souls,
We were ashamed of His presence
Near and Far,

He forgave us our Weakness,
Forgave us our lack of Compassion and
Our
Enability to *suffer with*

And

When our Hearts were consumed by infernos of Lust,
He drew merciful memories from the Maidens' Well
And hastily

Put
Us
Out

{Two-Beat Pause}

When we Hated,
He bestow'd Mercy

When we Coveted,
He uprooted our Passions and
Planted us anew

A Prince of Paradox,
He bestow'd Bronze upon us when we pray'd for Peace
And Peace when we call'd upon the Calamities of War

{One-Beat Pause}

And
When we,
En ignorance, sought the Ego

And perchance discover'd the hellhounds of Self-Loathing
Barking wildly at our doorsteps,
It was He who broke their fur-eed necks
With his strong hands
(Granting us safe passage *back* onto the Garten
Tyme and tyme again)

Brothas and Sistahs
He renewed us
He made us whole

He saved us from ourselves

And yet,
We did ev'rything en our Pow'r
To discourage, deceive, desert,
Discredit, denounce, and destroy Him!

We flogged the back of his thighs
With a rhinoceros' hide

And beat him steadily with our fists
Until all the cosmic oceans
And mystic rivers dried

These things we did and for
These things

We alone
Must atone

**[Thoughtlessly, Pastor Danville Sheds Water.
A Single Tear Falls From The Corner Of His Left Eye;
Aft Which,
His Black Blue Throat Is Again Fill'd With Brimstone.]**

Here!
Here lies the remnant of a mighty River
Whose mornings once flow'd

From the bluegrass of Kentucky
Thru the hills of Tennessee
Ento the red clay of Georgia

A River now stagnant
A River whose true purpose is all-but-forgotten
And ento which many throw the petals of dead flowers still

A River now toxic
A River now Avernus

Unfit for tireless Soul travel
Unfit for Bliss

Yet fit for baggage
Yet fit for chains

Yet fit
For infamy

No longer the pride of Judah
No longer a marvel
   . . . of the Nine Worlds

{One-Beat Pause}

Sons of Adam
Daughters of Eve

Here!
Here lies Roseland
Here lies the Great Chariot
        the Great Bear

Here lies Grandma (slowly
Letting down her hair)

Here!
Here lies ev'ry goddamned rainbow
Here lies ev'ry schoolyard kiss

      ev'ry kickball home run
      ev'ry swing
And miss!
       ev'ry pop
       ev'ry lock

Here lies Heartbreak
Here lies Sorrow

Here lies ev'ry risk taken (en haste)
      ev'ry ball of twine unraveled

      ev'ry roach clip
      ev'ry poor decision ever made

      ev'ry blue and pink candle on
      ev'ry birthday cake

      en the 5th fucking grade

{One-Beat Pause}

Brothas and Sistahs,
Eye say it!

Eye say it!
Eye say it!
Eye say it!

Here! Love lies and
Here it languishes

The Resolution of our eternal struggle,
Lifeless and cold

**[Pastor Danville's Trembling Right Hand Holds
Mightily The Right Side Of His Pulpit
While His Left Hand, Index Finger Extended,
Gestures Violently Toward The Stone Sarcophagus
Set Amidst His Negro Congregation.]**

This! This box
Is more than cruel mockery
It is a doom crafted by *OUR* mortal hands

[Pastor Danville Suddenly Resigned.]

Brothas and Sistahs,
The best of who and what we are
Has taken its leave

Here lies Love

Love is dead

Love has died

**[Shaking His Head, Pastor Danville Snaps Shut
The Jaws Of *The Herder's Tome*.]**

Hate to disappoint ya'll

{One-Beat Pause}

Hate to give ya cause to harp and groan (really, eye do)
cause to
Pleat yur brow and roll yur eyes (en utter disbelief)

[A Negro Congregation,
Fill'd With Discontent, Rumbles.]
What's this shit?
No Graces? No Goodwill?

No Happily-Ever-After?
No Magic Pill?

{Two-Beat Pause}

So

Sigh if ya haveta and
Spit if ya must

But like eye toldja en the beginning,
If ya'll came here

Half-expectin' this
Half-expectin' that

Ya'll gone leave God's House
With a sad and heavy heart

When the weight of my words
Comes crashing down around your ears

En the balcony!
{A Disheartening Groan From Pastor Danville's Negro
Congregation}
En the aisles!
{A Second Groan}
En the orchestra pit!
{A Third}

My words concerning this journey
                               this fantastic flight
(Ento a black, starless night); namely,

A parson's tale marred by cruelty, desolation, and fear

[Pastor Danville Smiling.]

Funny thing
En it, Love is protagonist, prophet, and trumpeter!

A beautiful Negro boy w/
   beautiful red lips and
   beautiful brown eyes, my dears

{Two-Beat Pause}

Irony of ironies

Here!

              [Pastor Danville Pleats His Brow.]

                      Here

         . . . is how the war will be won

How the War Was Won

A Fairy Tale

By Valentino Santi

These are mournful days, child -
Days filled with men who foolishly choose
To be more monster than god.

- Bera, age 88

If you see a spider,
Be brave, and squash it!

- Monae, age 4

THERE ONCE WAS A BEAUTIFUL MOUNTAIN at the center of the world and from the top of this mountain flowed Seven Rivers of great abundance and each river poured its riches into a village at the foot of the mountain. Because of these divine gifts, unselfishly bestowed, each of the seven villages enjoyed a measure of peace and prosperity ordinarily seen in the province of Dream. Every field of every village was bountiful at harvest. Every herd of cattle grew threefold. Every elder grew wise, not old. Every child was born healthy. Every marriage was strong. Every pantry was full of butter and every goatskin was fat with wine, cheer, and song.

This is how it was, generation after generation, age after age. Then, one day, in the Moon of the Lost Red Calf, the folk of every village took their lives and good fortune for granted. They forgot about the generosity of the rivers and the beauty of the mountain.

They became complacent and stopped caring for the fields.
They stopped caring for themselves and each other. They
became a selfish and paranoid lot. The old envied the
young. The young envied the old. Fathers envied their sons
and clerics coveted the daughters of their congregations.
Wives hated their husbands. Husbands hated their Wives.
Magistrates became tyrants and merchants became roadside
thieves.

That's when a Serpent appeared on the mountain. It was
small, a little bitty thing, hardly anything at all. It nearly
went unnoticed until a milliner, gin drunk, caught sight of it
through a crack in his garden wall. Not content with its
small stature, the Serpent grew and grew and grew. It grew
until its hold on the mountain startled a camp of lazy
cowherds. It grew until, coiled stubbornly around the
mountain, the once mighty rush of the Seven Rivers
resembled the feeble streams of a broken beer tap.

In time, the Serpent grew strong enough to hold back every drop of every river's flow and the villages at the foot of the mountain became acres of dying peach trees, barren cows, and sickly children. Indeed, the Serpent took hold of the mountain and a curse took hold of every village and every heart. This is how it was, generation after generation, age after age. The people blasphemed the gods and set fire to their sacred groves. They held responsible the gods for their troubles. They held their clerics. They held their neighbors. They held their kings and kings' men but never did they *hold themselves* responsible for their plight. All the while, starvation, thirst, and disease held sway over their lives and the lives of their children and grandchildren.

Early one morning, a godless Archer appeared. He had not a shining breastplate to thump. He had not a white horse to saddle. He had not papers of knightly descent to declare. He had not a bless-ed crest to display.

Only the holes in his boots spoke frankly of his modest lineage and long, arduous journey from a rabbit's hole to a mountain at the center of the world. Neither the Archer's sudden appearance nor his silver bow (a bow called Truth) and bear pelt quiver (a quiver called Tridevi) eased the villagers' troubled minds. 14,000 mortals and 14,000 devas had, over the ages, sought to slay the Serpent, free the waters, and restore the lands, but to no avail. So, the villagers, wary of hope, expected much of the same from any effort put forth by the Archer.

Well acquainted with his role as hero and the task that lay before him, the Archer did not stop to contemplate the suffering folk or the rare color of the sky above his head. Lo! The Archer is a hero and a hero acts. He acts without remorse, without guilt, and his acts are clean and sweet (like the waters he seeks to release).

The Archer struck first. Standing on a little patch of
parched red clay, he blindly fed his bow an arrow from his
quiver. Parvati (the arrow was called), though shining fair,
flew unseen. She hit her mark and staked the Serpent's
cagey tail to the mountain.

Wounded, the Serpent thrashed and the thrashing shook the
sky and shattered every Rose window in every cathedral in
every village square. The unearthly clamor drew the
attention of every cowherd in every village with ears to
hear and eyes to see.

Under attack, the Serpent set his narrow eyes firmly upon
the Archer. His scales bristled at the thought of bloody
reprisal. Undaunted by the Serpent's retaliatory stance, the
Archer again raised his weapon to strike. The second arrow
he fed his bow was entirely of his choosing. Smirking, he
closed his left eye and cast his right over the Serpent's

powerful body. From the heavens, a ray of light fell upon the tip of the arrow's head and promptly revealed the target to the Archer. Lakshmi (the arrow was called), atop that ray of light, flew. She hit her mark and staked the Serpent's belly to the mountain.

Nearly split-in-twain, the Serpent opened its mouth and exposed its giant white fangs and forked tongue. It hissed angrily and unfurled its vast hood. The Archer was not moved by the Serpent's anguish. He was not moved by its spectacle, its garish display of terror and intent to drive him from his spot - his little patch of parched red clay. Loud and clear, the Archer spoke, "The others fell prey to your charms; but eye will not. Not here, not now, not today."

A rare smile crept across the Archer's sweet face as he fed his silver bow and growled; and on the back of that growl Saraswati (the arrow was called) flew, the third and last arrow in his quiver. She hit her mark and staked the Serpent's flashing red tongue to the mountain. The arrows, unlike the Archer, were sympathetic. The Serpent's torment moved them and they dispensed grace. The Serpent turned to solid stone (it would not feel the final blow). It was a feat worthy of Medusa's brow.

On bended knee, Eye touch the Earth and call her to bear witness when a cruel, almost crippling pain, rips thru me. Eye look down at my left hand. My left forefinger is sliced open and dripping blood. Eye watch amazed as my Life's wine slowly seeps ento a little patch of parched red clay.

The Archer stood, kicked the dirt at his heels, and discovered the root of his injury - the gilded head of a fabled spear still intact, a spear from the old god wars. He drew the spear from the earth beneath his boots, gripped it tightly in his bleeding left hand, steadied himself, and, with a wink, hurled it at the stone Serpent coiled around the World Mountain.

Ushas (the spear was called) struck the creature's head. Its powerful body quivered suddenly and then broke into a thousand pieces; after which, a thousand torrents of water poured forth. The villages were consumed and every cow, garden, and trellis was restored.

The Seven Rivers from the top of the mountain once again flowed freely. Peace and prosperity ordinarily seen in the province of Dream returned to the villages and the folk never again took their lives and good fortune for granted.

The Archer died in the deluge but he was not forgotten. From the little patch of parched red clay where he bravely stood and his blood spilt, bloomed a brilliant plot of archer's gold.

Seven maidens, one from each village, each one left-handed and each one more beautiful than the next, tended the plot daily. This is how it was and how it will be, generation after generation, age after age. A paradise restored, a people reborn, and a hero revered.

Fin

www.ingramcontent.com/pod-product-compliance
Lightning Source LLC
Chambersburg PA
CBHW021018180626
46814CB00003B/1337